The Poverty of Good Portions

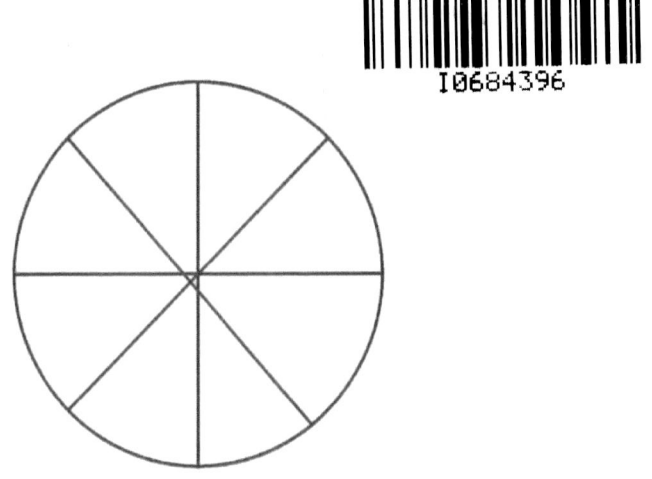

J. Friedrich Allyn

This is a work of fiction. Any similarity to any real life individual, event, or action is purely coincidental.

Cover art by J. Friedrich Allyn

Send all inquiries to: BlackCouchLounge@protonmail.com

First printing, 2019
Second printing, 2021

ISBN-13: 978-1-7340542-9-3

For all the men who have betrayed themselves.

Please be advised:

The description and narratives of degraded human states is not to be ingested lightly.

When reading these stories you will be confronted with moments in the lives of young men that are of a secretive nature and kept very private. These stories not only seek an understanding of the mechanics of these occurrences, but also attempt to showcase a perspective to the reader on aspects of men and boys that is often deeply misunderstood.

Note on 2nd Edition:

When I first published *The Poverty of Good Portions* in 2019 the world was very different. Not just the world at large, but my personal world as well. In fact, when I began writing and organizing these stories, some as early as 2013, the two worlds were different all the more. The current year is 2021, and I'm on the cusp of publishing my second work, *On The Waves of An Odyssey,* and I found myself re-reading Poverty.

I did this in an effort to 1) see if it needed any updates, 2) see if the stories still resonated and communicated what I intended to communicate, and 3) take it in with an expanded sense of the reader, based on all the feedback I've received over the last couple of years.

On the first, there were really only a couple of grammatical and formatting changes, which is no surprise since I technically didn't learn to spell properly until I was almost 30 years old.

On the second, I was humbled and pleased that I still felt the stories relevant to what I wanted to communicate. That's not to say they are perfect, or that some authors haven't done similar themes in a more eloquent or thorough way, but from my personal standpoint I still wouldn't have written it any differently.

On the third, I got a deeper sense of some of the criticism I've received. I don't agree with all of it, but I believe I understand more of what the reader of such stories is looking for. I have since begun asking any would-be reader that I encounter to "find something to criticize" as not only does this make me a better writer, but it gives the reader full permission to be honest. Good writers seek truth and it's only right that we be able to also receive the truth. After all, if we can't accept the truth, then we have no business claiming to speak the truth.

This book still seeks truth and makes no apologies, and I am still very proud of this work.

Contents

A Most Unlucky Sailor

The boys were vicious. Jonah was physically smaller than the others, but his personality was the most dominant; some call this a Napoleon complex. He led the others in their taunts and bullying in school, his forceful bravado often creating a tension in the air suggesting he could benefit from chaos under the right circumstances. Jonah had not yet refined his persuasive confidence to push others past mere posturing and light violence, but he was learning.

One particularly cloudy Sunday, Jonah and the boys were attempting to skate some equipment at the construction site behind the school. The new athletic and aquatic center was in the process of being built and they took advantage of this isolated and impromptu skate park, enjoying some stolen beer, and talking of ways to score weed or get some girls to meet up. Ultimately, they ended up just sitting on their boards by the curb flicking rocks and talking shit.

The construction crew was often neglectful and would leave equipment and tools out in the open, barely protected by a flimsy and unsecure gate. They spent the latter half of their 10th grade year lurking around the unfinished building, playing king of the mountain on the dirt hills, carving obscenities into the weak cement, and engaging in generally delinquent behavior; the construction site was their haven and hangout.

Lightening appeared overhead, followed by a low rumble 10 seconds later. It was going to start raining soon and the build site would puddle and flood. The construction crew had dug trenches for pipes connecting what was to become an Olympic size diving pool. Another series of tanks and reservoirs would be installed to constantly cycle and filter the pool water. Supposedly, this design would make the facility less wasteful and more ecofriendly but the validity of this claim was yet to be proven. The dangers of the open site were apparent to any adult who took the time to look but none did.

Another boy, a new and somewhat quiet 9th grader, also named Jonah, came skating down the sidewalk with excitement in his eyes. He had become somewhat enamored with the group because of how cool they appeared. The elder Jonah in particular held his interest, in part because he had never met another boy with his name. He also liked skateboarding so it seemed only natural that they should be friends. Unfortunately, what was exciting to young Jonah was annoying to the elder.

"Ah shit, here's the faggot Jonah coming to play with the big kids again." One of the boys remarked.

"Don't call him that", Jonah snapped, "It's my name and no one else's."

Elder Jonah had also never met another boy with his name and he felt this new kid diminished his reputation and status because of the shared title. It didn't matter if the new kid was much cooler, smarter, more dangerous, or even the biggest nerd of all; another Jonah muddied his name and reputation; caused a ripple in his persona.

"We should figure out another name for him then, fix his parents stupidity," said another of the boys, seeking favor.

Jonah smirked. This could be fun, he thought.

"Hey guys! Any cool new skate set ups today?!" Young Jonah shouted with a naive enthusiasm starkly contrasted with the older boys.

"Yeah, but they're ours." One of the boys shot back. The others snickered.

"Oh." Young Jonah stood still and thought for a moment. He felt an unwelcome air but didn't have enough experience to interpret it as such.

"Hey kid, you got a middle name?" Elder Jonah asked sharply.

"Yeah, but I don't like it. I much prefer my first name, don't you?" Young Jonah replied. A personal question made him forget his uneasy feeling.

"Yeah, I do, that's the point. The name is mine, and no one else's. So, it's either you tell us your middle name or we make one up for you".

"Like what?" Young Jonah asked, feeling hopeful at the notion of inclusion.

"Like queer-bait, fuck-face, or cum-stain. You know, the usual terms of affection." The group all laughed aloud, more so from the tension created at the taunt than from any of Jonah's cleverness.

"I don't like those names." Young Jonah said, the uneasy feeling returning.

"Exactly, that's why we need to know your middle name, so we don't have to hurt your queer little feelings." Elder Jonah said aggressively before easing back into a smirk, confident that his manipulation was working.

"Hmm, can't there just be two Jonah's?" Young Jonah asked meekly.

"No. You don't get to have my name." Elder Jonah said, becoming irritated.

"I think I need to go home; my mom is probably wondering where I am." Young Jonah said, turning around quickly to escape.

Elder Jonah shot up from the curb and the other boys followed suit. For a passing moment, Elder Jonah noticed the others in lock step with his movements and felt a pride in the power he had cultivated.

"No, no, no, no you don't." Elder Jonah said a sneer.

"Yeah, don't be rude, we're in the middle of a conversation here." Another boy chimed in as they all circled around Young Jonah, cutting off his departure.

Thunder rumbled again almost at the same moment Elder Jonah laid his hands on Young Jonah's shoulders to pin him in place. Elder

Jonah stared Young Jonah in the eyes for a moment and could see the fear building. Then he looked up a bit and flicked Young Jonah's awkward bike helmet with his fingers. "Your mom make you wear that when you go out to skate, cum-wad?"

Young Jonah was too afraid to answer back. He just stared wide-eyed with confusion. The boys began to laugh at his silence and participated in the exchange, joking that it was a good thing rain was starting so he could hide when he started pissing his pants later.

"I'll take that as a yes." Elder Jonah said, and yanked on Young Jonah's brand new wallet chain, pulling the wallet out of his back pocket.

"Hey, that's mine!" Young Jonah shouted in a shrill voice.

"Shut up!" Elder Jonah shouted back, mocking the shrillness. The boys all laughed. "I just want to see what your ID card says".

Young Jonah tried to grab his wallet back but one of the boys slapped his hand down and another shoved his chest, pushing him into a third. Young Jonah gave in quickly and quietly, frowning at his treatment, his lower lip shaking lightly.

"Jonah Odyss... what the actual fuck does that say?" Elder Jonah said with a laugh. "Your parents are fucking weird. I would hate that name too, but it's perfect for you."

Young Jonah's face changed from frightened to angry in an instant. He instinctively knew this was only going to become the name everyone at school called him from now on. It would also be the source of endless taunting unless he was able to do something about it.

It started to rain a bit now, and more thunder was heard; the lightning was going to be right over them in a few minutes.

Young Jonah's anger flared and he lunged forward in a rage. Elder Jonah didn't see this coming and took a solid punch right in the jaw, causing him to step back in surprise. Young Jonah's fear returned as he realized that he wasn't nearly strong enough to win this fight, no matter how short the Elder was.

Elder Jonah smirked and nodded a bit accepting the escalation. He then took a step forward and slapped the Younger hard across the face, knocking him down onto the damp muddy ground. Thunder struck again as Young Jonah scrambled to his feet and tried to make a run for it through the crowd of boys.

The other boys were taller, stronger, and faster so he only made it a few yards. One of the boys was able to tackle him easily without even going down to the ground himself, spilling Young Jonah face first onto the ground. The visor-like point on the front of Young Jonah's bike helmet scraped through the mud and gravel, creating a small trench that buried his face. He rolled over with his face covered in mud and his nose bleeding.

"Oooooo" the boys all moaned in unison impressed with the impact of the takedown.

"What are you running for? Can't stay and finish what you started Oddy boy?" Thunder stuck once more and the rain picked up; it was going to downpour soon.

"I told you I don't like that name!" Young Jonah screamed through his teeth, visibly shaking with anger and humiliation.

"So, what, you just going to sit there in the mud and cry about it or are you going to get up and finish what you started?" Elder Jonah taunted.

Young Jonah got to his feet, ready to attack again, when one of his shoes came off, caught in the thick mud of a puddle, and caused him to fall to the ground once more. The boys couldn't contain their howls of laughter as young Jonah fumbled around trying to dislodge his shoe, growing filthier in the process. He began to cry.

"This is just pathetic now." Elder Jonah said, growing bored. "I have an idea though."

It had now begun to rain more consistently. The half-finished piping system was beginning to show signs of functionality as the rain picked up. The boys often liked to put trash and other objects into the pipes to see where the exits were, often making outlandish bets on the outcome that they never seriously intended to pay.

Elder Jonah took a quick look around and found the largest of all the pips angled 45 degrees out of the mud. He had always thought it looked like a water slide of sorts and had tried to get one of the other boys to take a ride but they were too big; they were also afraid of being stuck. Young Jonah wasn't all that big, surely, he would fit.

Elder Jonah gestured, "See that pipe over there? I bet young Odders here would fit fine."

"Yeah, I bet so too!" said one of the other boys excitedly.

"Hey Odysissy, since you're all muddy we're going to do you a favor and clean you up before sending you back to you mom."

"NO!" Young Jonah screeched in panic. He had a mild fear of enclosed spaces and he also wasn't going to just take being bullied if could get away. He tried to get up and run again, but short one shoe and covered in mud he was slower than before. It took no time for two of the boys to grab and carry him up into the air, kicking and screaming all the way over to the pipes opening.

Elder Jonah smacked the top of his helmet, "Now the question is, before we give you a bath like the little baby that you are, is do you want to go in feet first or head first?"

"Neither!" Put me down you motherfuckers!" Young Jonah screamed and struggled to loosen himself.

"Whoa, such language from someone in such a weak position, maybe, Odysucks-cock, we can teach you to respect your elders."

"Go to hell, you midget piece of shit!"

"Yeah, you definitely need a lesson. As your elder, I know what's best, and I say... headfirst! After all, you're wearing that stylish helmet and it'll likely break your fall when you go shooting out the other end. Thoughtful right?"

Elder Jonah took a quick look down into the unfinished pool of water rising in the rain and could already see water coming out the other end. "I bet you guys $100 he shoots out like a torpedo into the air before making a huge splash."

"Yeah just like a torpedo!" The boys laughed, turned young Jonah's feet up in the air. They rested the back of his helmet on the edge of the pipe, forced his hands into the pockets of his jeans, and gave him a heavy push.

Young Jonah began his freefall through the pipe with a scream. He couldn't see because of the darkness of the pipe and he couldn't hear anything but the rush of air and water. He felt the first angle of the pipe on his shoulders as he landed with a sharp jolt. The slide became a bit slower but not much. He was able to catch his bearings in that moment and pull his hands free from his pockets though he was unable move his arms from his side or slow his plummet.

Suddenly he came to a painful stop against his helmet. There wasn't yet enough water to engulf him but he also couldn't open his eyes with all of it running up his face. He knew he was no longer falling but with each attempt to catch his breath, he gagged on the silty water. He began to take panicked breaths and wiggle furiously in the limited space. Suddenly, his wiggling caused the freefall to continue for another brief moment. The pipe had shrunk even more and the visor on his helmet had halted his fall against the pipe, this time the visor bending forward over his brow.

He lay face up in the darkness, arms unable to reach his face. More panicked breathing came as his helmet, now wedging him firmly in the pipe, began to fill with water. He could even see little shards of light breaking through around him, indicating that he was at the opening of the pipe, almost out.

He couldn't open his eyes and he couldn't touch his face. His body and helmet acting as a plug, the water slowly rose to the corners of his nostrils. It tipped the sides into his nasal cavity and burned with surprise. He lurched up clearing the water line for a moment. As he fell back down his face was engulfed; the water now pouring into his mouth.

Before Young Jonah was able to scream, water had filled his sinuses and his gag reflex caused him to expel the remaining air from his lungs. He was unable to exhale or inhale without aspirating water. Due to his elevated position, his lungs did not immediately fill with water but instead caused a quickened, repeated asphyxiation in intervals between longer bursts resulting in complete panic and terror. In this moment, all Young Jonah could think was how he hated his mom for making him wear the helmet.

Lightening stuck over the construction site. The boys up above, soaking wet, looked on, all shifting uneasily, a growing pain in their guts. They couldn't see the opening of the pipe but they could all see that Young Jonah didn't fire out like a torpedo. The air around them changed and all were silent.

Elder Jonah became acutely aware of the gravity of situation. His persona dropped, and he looked slowly to the boy next to him, swallowed hard, and in a hushed and fearful voice said, "w-what do we do?"

Fractured Mosaic

There was always this vague mistrust in the air, the kind that is never spoken because both parties are just insecure enough about their mistrust that they wonder if it's mostly in their head.

Julian remained unconvinced that his intuition was wrong about the cause of his own insecurity on the matter, and was so absolutely full of conviction that he was constantly looking for clues to prove his fears correct.

Zoe was very naturally solipsistic, and tended to live more in the clouds than on the ground. Her lack of experience outside of herself was no match for his experience observing the behavior of others, weak though it was. If asked, he could admit to a pronounced blind spot within his own romantic situations.

As they sat watching movies late into the evening, her lounging provocatively, yet somehow innocently in over worn black underwear, knee high socks, and a sweater. Julian remained oblivious to the TV, and couldn't seem to keep his eyes off her cell phone sitting face up on the coffee table; he was racked with anxiety. It was as if the evidence he was waiting on, and knew existed, would suddenly appear there in bold letters, and sing truth into the air. His desire for the truth was so strong that her continued vague and varied sexual posturing had no effect on him.

Eventually, a text did appear, but it was too far away to read. Julian tensed. She didn't move to reach for the phone immediately, but when he leaned forward to spy a look, pretending to reach for his wine, she leaned forward in unison. The name *Jason* was all he could see.

Who was Jason? And why was there no last name showing? He thought. He knew how meticulous she was about filling out the contact info of everyone she knew, yet this was just a first name. Jason. Nothing else to know aside from the fact it was a man and he was sending lengthy texts to Julian's lover late in the night. He tensed again, but said nothing.

She laid the phone back down, still face up, and leaned back calmly without a word, as if Julian wasn't exploding with torment on the inside. His mind rapid-fired rationalizations for all his fears, but couldn't shake the fact that this was a new person-a new man-in her life, and they had not become familiar enough to exchange further information.

He couldn't pull his focus from the matter. *Was Jason an irrelevant association? A passing flirtation? Just an inconsiderate but otherwise innocent coworker? Maybe he was quick sexual outlet for when she became bored with me?* Another text came through, piercing his thoughts.

This time Julian remained still and pretended not to see, and she shifted her legs into a strange position that seemed to block him from seeing the phone lighting up on the table, but also made sure she contacted him physically. *Was that on purpose?* he thought, annoyed at her physical touch in this moment.

She didn't reach for the phone, and another couple of minutes went by. Julian leaned forward again for his wine, and the phone lit up again.

"Your phone is blowing up over here." He finally managed to blurt out, far too loudly to seem natural. She jumped up immediately to grab it. He still only saw the name. Jason.

Julian leaned back and looked out of the side of his eye at her fast typing. He has an iPhone, evidenced from the blue text bubbles, and he's using the smirking devil face emoji, but the words are still too far to make out properly. She finishes her reply and set the phone back on the table frustrated and with irritation, this time face down.

Say something, he thought.

"Who you texting?" Julian asked, trying to sound playful. Instead, he came across just as emotionally charged and panicked as he felt. If she detected the emotion in his voice, she ignored it.

"Oh, just one of my old roommates, the ones that just had a kid."

Shit, he thought, *I don't remember that guy's name, and it could be anything, even Jason. Maybe I'm being paranoid.*

"Oh, what do they want?"

"Nothing special, just checking in."

Julian always hated that phrase, checking in. It reminded him of his grandmother and so many others he had known that ignored linguistic patterns and the meaning of words. It was as if they remained unaware of people and things outside their own feelings, or were otherwise lacking in wider consciousness. He reasoned that this behavior was born out of the need to feel secure in the fact that they're not actively involved in a person's life, but feel somehow responsible for the emotional state of the person they're inquiring about, and further feel guilty for not tending to the relationship more closely.

He reasoned that checking in was half out of the hope that something was wrong or amiss so that they can become more involved. A justification for selfishly inserting themselves in another's life under the guise of caring. All moms have this characteristic in some degree, and Julian found it fussy and nosy. Zoe, even though without children, was fully possessed by this tendency at times, making the phrase checking in a common parlance even when she wasn't the one checking in.

Julian shook off this minor annoyance and remained silent, settling back into the awful grey area between insecurity of his mistrusted intuition and the absolute conviction that his rationalizations were sound. The tension in this space was exhausting but familiar.

They continued watching the film. Julian eventually began to relax and joke around due to the alcohol; denial has a certain comfort. They eventually listened to some music, smoked some weed, and fell asleep after having sex, which was noticeably rougher than usual.

Later in the evening, Julian awoke with a start to the sound of Zoe snoring loudly. He had recently read an article about how sleeping on your left side was healthier and he was attempting it this night. Forming this habit was not comfortable and as a result, he was easily awakened. He lay still for a moment, listening to her snore. His mind drifted back to Jason, who he was, and if anything about it should be expressed. In an instant he decided that he needed to know more before broaching the subject. He seized the opportunity provided by the cover of night, and slipped into the living room to see if any more messages had come through on her phone.

He found her phone still face down, in the same place she had left it before, and felt a reassurance that she hadn't paid any more attention to the phone after her last message. This almost stopped him from going further but he was riding the wave; there were two messages:

"Oh, c'mon, help a brother out!" 1:28am

"Out of sight, out of mind I guess." 1:35am

Julian stood still, petrified with anger and hurt. He hated being right about this. However, his feelings quickly swirled into confusion as he realized there was nothing explicit in these messages, he couldn't prove anything, just vaguely implied sexual relations and an acknowledgement that since she wasn't with him, she must not care to think about him. That's often how Julian felt too; out of her sight, out of her mind.

His emotions landed on something solid and he thought *who uses the phrase* "help a brother out?" *Some loser that shouldn't even be a consideration, much less competition for her!* He thought, jealousy surging.

He wanted to open the phone and search for more context but he didn't have the lock code. Even if he did, she would see that she had unread messages without alerts, a dead giveaway that he had invaded her privacy. Instead, he took to her Facebook to see if she knew anyone named Jason. She knew one, a gay man in Canada, which didn't provide evidence in any helpful direction. He was at a loss and began to feel guilty for his snooping. He went back to bed and tried to put it out of his mind, entering Zoe in her sleep in a desperate attempt to gain some control over her and the situation brewing in his mind. She didn't mind when he did this. She never minded.

The next morning was fairly playful and carefree with more sex before getting out of bed. Julian was sitting on the floor facing the toilet and trimming his shaggy beard into the bowl when he heard Zoe in the other room cussing about something.

"What is it? I can't hear you." Julian said loudly. Zoe entered the bathroom phone in hand.

Oh shit, Julian thought bracing himself for an ass chewing.

"My old roommate apparently sent me some texts asking for nude photos since Anna is still recovering from her pregnancy."

Julian's eyes went large, staring straight into the large pile of matted hair floating in the toilet. *Is she really going to try to swing her lies into a web of half-truths just to minimize my suspicions? Does she know I looked and is now pulling damage control? Is she telling the truth?* Julian had no idea what to believe, so he just maintained his shaving task, and asked her questions, partly to hide his feelings from her, and partly to gain more information.

"The one you were texting last night?"

"Yea, the ones you've met a couple of times when we first met. Remember Jason and Anna?"

Julian still couldn't remember if that was the guy's name, but at this point, he had to take Zoe at her word on that. She was committed to selling it.

"Oh, yeah. Has he ever done that before? Did you ever fool around with him?"

"No. What? No, he's been caught a couple of times talking inappropriately to other girls, but never caught actually doing anything physical, and he's never done it with me."

"What did you reply back?"

"Nothing, I don't know what to say."

Julian still wasn't sure if this was all an act for his benefit or the truth and he was already becoming exhausted from the conversation. She gave nothing away outside of the possibility of the situation being too absurd to be taken seriously.

"Hm, well let me see the text and maybe I can help."

"I deleted it already."

"What? No, you didn't! Girls don't delete texts, especially when they're mad about them" he said, annoyed at how stupid she must believe him to be.

"I did! I don't want to look at it or know it happened, I just want to ignore it." She said, walking quickly into the other room.

This was more dramatic a response than necessary. "So why are you huffing and puffing to me about it then?"

"I don't know. I just feel comfortable expressing myself to you! Maybe I shouldn't," she said meekly.

Julian rolled his eyes. He forced down the urge to call her out on her ruse, and proceeded to placate the fear of his own feelings, and take up the yoke of her not being fulfilled emotionally. He sat silently, looking at the toilet seat. After a moment, Zoe cut the silence by asking what he wanted for lunch. The subject of her text messages never came up again for the rest of the day. It was never far from his mind though.

Later in bed, Julian lay reading and stopped to marvel at his ability to distract himself from paralyzing self-doubt. He felt sad and confused, like he wasn't being as good a man as he should be. They had been involved for a year and it was the best sex he had ever had, but it had happened way too fast. When he became suspicious of her fooling around, he would often think back to how he wished he had waited a while to get to know her better.

He knew that she held the power in their relationship due to the sexual nature of all their exchanges. It was so easy for her to distract and arouse him, and given how she much she loved being choked, slapped, and generally abused during sex, he always felt tremendous relief afterwards on many levels, and promptly forgot what was bothering him beforehand.

This situation was a big deal to him though, and based on her behavior in the morning, she was invested in him for some reason. Julian just didn't believe what she told him. He didn't trust her and strangely he didn't want to, and he wondered if not wanting to believe her meant that he didn't want to be with her at all. He felt certain these feelings showed glaringly on his face and wondered if she noticed.

He looked over to see her sleeping soundly and just stared for a moment. She wasn't beautiful, but she was very cute, and he preferred cute to beautiful for some reason. In his more honest moments, he could admit that he was easily intimidated by beautiful women and the powerful confidence that tended to accompany them. Cute was an easier affect to manage and allowed him to feel more in control.

She woke up, looked at him looking at her, forced a smile, and got up to pee when he heard a phone vibrate on the counter in the kitchen. His ears perked and his skin tingled. I have to see what that is while I have the chance, he thought.

When he got to the kitchen where their phones were plugged up, he sighed seeing that it was his phone that vibrated with a text from a friend across the country. Apparently, his friend had forgotten the time difference. He decided not to answer the text as it would just lead to a lengthy conversation and he really needed some sleep.

He hesitated, looking at Zoë's phone plugged in and lying face down on the counter. *I could look again. I shouldn't though. I already violated her trust once. I don't want to make it a habit. If I'm right though, then she is violating my trust too. If I'm right, would it matter?*

With that, he seized her phone and hit the button to illuminate the screen; nothing was there. He felt like an ass but also felt relief. *No news is good news I guess,* he thought, taking on a similar attitude as Jason the previous night, rationalizing in order to dismiss the situation.

He climbed back in bed. Zoe had already returned. He snuggled up behind, and she responded by pulling him into her with a satisfied, half-sleepy moan. They lay this way for a few moments when her eyes shot open and she turned to face him as if he had just slapped her in public.

"What's wrong?" She asked, brow furrowed, now fully awake.

"Nothing, why do you think something is wrong?" Julian said, sounding defensive.

"Oh, usually when you wrap up behind me it's not long before you're inside me. I can't even feel if you're hard right now."

Julian was taken aback for a moment, looked away in thought, and was about to speak when he felt her hands slide into his waistband and caress his groin, initiating an erection. He was startled into eye contact and she smiled knowingly.

"Good, there you are, I was about to get worried I had lost all my charm." She said as she turned around and positioned herself against him.

Julian frowned at first, inhaled, and grumbled "not at all", and followed through. Dutifully. Just like every time before.

Organic Orbits

I met Mark a couple of years ago randomly at a punk rock show. We were the only two people who didn't have a good time. Turns out, we had much in common and since being out of college for a couple of years, the opportunities of making new friends had become more difficult, and both of us relished the chance meeting.

Our relationship consisted mostly of drinking, playing music, eating late into the night and causing a ruckus in the local bars and strip clubs; Mark would even end up sleeping with a stripper or two due to my charming wingman abilities. I didn't care to sleep with strippers but was happy to help out a friend. I was always more of a relationship type of guy anyway, but due to my lifestyle I had always attracted the wrong types of women, which is annoying to say the least. In fact, the deeper you become ingrained into a certain type of back and forth with a certain type of woman it becomes harder to have meaningful rapport with what might be the right type.

Anyway, one evening we were out with one such female friend, a very cute, gregarious Mexican girl named Marisol. We had become friends in an English Literature class in college when I very kindly offered to help her with any English trouble she may encounter. She didn't really need the help but also didn't say no, which encouraged me, and, since I am fairly handsome and had other handsome friends, it was an attractive association for her too. I was smitten with Marisol in an almost pathetic way. Strike that, there was no 'almost' about it.

The night was going smoothly, and though I knew Mark was attracted to Marisol, I didn't feel any threat or jealousy since I trusted his friendship and also because she was very vocal about remaining a virgin till marriage; I totally would have waited for her.

"Guys, serious question, and I don't want you to feel any obligation, but a guy I work with sold me some really great weed and I have some shrooms I've been wanting to get into; any interest?" Mark was full of surprises.

"Oh my gosh reeaallly? I've never done shrooms before!" Marisol exclaimed eyes wide. I observed her thoughtfully, her cliché Latina mannerisms were so cute.

"Oh, it's really something, and it's a good idea for your first time to be in the company of someone experienced." Mark said.

"Asa, have you ever done it? Would you want to?" Marisol asked.

"I could be down with that; I've smoked a couple times but never done shrooms."

"Oh dude, it's the best, and I can promise that mixed with the pot you'll definitely get some visual hallucinations." Mark's confidence was intoxicating.

"Ok, let's do it. Your place?" I asked.

"No, my sister and her boyfriend are in town visiting my folks and I'm letting them have the run of my place, how about yours?"

"Let's go to my place, my roommate isn't there and I have lots of wine!" Marisol cried out showing her excitement.

"Sounds good to me, I need to stop by my place and pick it up then I'll meet you guys at Marisol's, just text me the address."

I was more excited at the prospect of staying at Marisol's house than the drugs at this point.

Marisol lived in an old college dorm style apartment where each tenant had their own bedroom and bathroom but a shared living space. There were currently only two tenants but it could have held four. These kinds of places were built with the idea that no one would stay very long and would likely destroy a good portion of it, and they were cheap for downtown; perfect for college kids. She had been here for six years at this point, mostly because she didn't want to go back to Mexico. She just stayed in school in order to take full advantage of her immigrant status.

When we arrived, she knocked on her roommate's door just to check that she was gone and found no answer. "Ok good. She's a real bitch about me having people over so I don't want to deal with all that."

"Didn't you say you had some wine?"

"Yes! I also have some tequila, should we take a shot before Mark arrives?"

"You read my mind."

We took two shots, shuffled through her music, and ended up playing some Italian house music that made Marisol dance like the kids in old Woodstock footage. I watched her move with a lustful intensity but looked away whenever her eyes landed on me. I hated myself for being so afraid of her, but I didn't know how to control the urge to look away.

Mark showed up like a hip-hop star to a club, arms up, and hands full. Marisol gave a light clap with an excited smile. He set a small gym bag on the table and produced a machine that looked like a large salad spinner and then a coffee can that was clearly older than anyone in the room.

"I brought my vaporizer; it's the best way to smoke."

"What's in the coffee can?"

"That's the stuff. I found this can in my dad's garage when I was a teenager and it was the first time I had ever seen pot and I've used it ever since. My dad thought I accidentally tossed it cleaning one day."

"Very cool."

"What's she up to? Is she already high?"

"No, we did a couple of shots but given that she's less than 100lbs she may already be drunk."

"Hah, well, load me up some shots to catch up and I'll portion this stuff out." He said as he loaded up his vaporizer and laid out what looked to be small chocolate bars on the table.

"OK, Marisol, come over here and listen for a minute!" Mark shouted.

"Mark!" Marisol screamed and jumped to give him a hug. I winched a bit, and started to feel a bit jealous, the arousal I had from watching her dance not yet fully deflated.

"Ok, so before we take the shrooms let's all take a couple of hits as a way to prime the pump, so to speak." Mark said, handing Marisol the pipe end of a tube.

"What's with the chocolate?" I asked. "Those are the shrooms. They're coated in chocolate so the taste isn't so bad. That reminds me though, I'm going to need $20 from each of you for the shrooms and I'll consider the alcohol a fair trade for the pot." Mark said with complete seriousness.

"Oh, you're charging us? Kind of wish you had said that beforehand. You're lucky I even have cash on me." That motherfucker, I was understandably a bit insulted but understood that the shrooms were likely not cheap. Marisol had danced away after taking a large hit of the vaporizer and didn't hear this exchange so naturally I paid for her too.

"Sweet. Dude, let's hit up that balcony for a few minutes while the THC gets into our system." Mark said, already moving toward the sliding door.

"Marisol! We're going on the balcony!" I shouted over the dance music.

"Ok! I'll find a good chill song and join you."

The balcony was small but over looked a small park, which was illuminated by the new moon in the clear sky. We stood still for a moment and remarked on how pretty it was and how nice the autumn air felt. We sat in the deck chairs and just stared out, both of us fully relaxed and enjoying the wind, the rocking of the chairs, and the stillness of the night.

I suddenly became aware of Marisol's absence, like I was jarred out of trance by something, "What is she doing in there? How much time has passed?"

"Haha, I don't know and I don't know man, but I think we're ready for that chocolate now. Are you feeling good?"

"Yeah man, I'm fucking lit."

We got up slowly, with difficulty and laughed at ourselves. We reentered the apartment to see Marisol on her knees in front of an iPod mounted to a stereo on the floor, scrolling through songs using the tracking method so she was hearing all the songs being played at 10 times the normal speed, and she found this hysterical. No wonder I was suddenly jarred out of my trance, this was an obnoxious sound.

"Marisol, you kook, what're you doing?"

"Asa, oh my god, can you hear this, it's incredible. I didn't know I could hear music this fast!"

"That's wild," Mark said, "are you ready for the shrooms?" Marisol looked up, pupils already solid black, and nodded enthusiastically in agreement.

"Cool, hang tight. Asa, she is already geeked out from the weed, I'm thinking we only give her half just to be safe."

"Good idea, and we can split her half." Mark was surprisingly held together compared to us, and I suddenly couldn't' recall him actually taking a hit of the weed himself, surely he had though.

"This is why we're friends, you're always so thoughtful." Mark said with a smile.

We broke one of the chocolates in half and then chewed up our own portions. I gagged at the taste and was immediately thankful for the chocolate; Mark began to laugh and had a hard time stopping, so he must have taken a hit after all. I took Marisol's portion to her and she was back in front of the iPod scrolling songs again. She ate it out of my hand, wetting my fingers, and chewed it up without even looking away, she didn't' seem to notice the awful taste, all physical stimulation processing power occupied with the visual. I lingered a minute due to her scent and the fact that I had felt a part of her in such a sensation heavy way.

I spun out of that sensation and Mark and I returned to the balcony and melted away into the wind-blown tracers blending the leaves of the trees with the lights of the city. After a few minutes neither of us could stand up and would occasionally laugh at our attempts. This is when things started to get really weird for me; I'm certain that Mark began to communicate with me telepathically.

I couldn't be sure if it was something Mark was doing on purpose or if I was suddenly able to know the meaning and intent behind all of Mark's actions and his body moments. Maybe his unconscious was seeping through to me. I was unable to focus on anything else outside of him and his attempt at words but I was certain that something was being communicated and it was important.

I remember that I just stared at him with a peculiar intensity and if you asked me then, I wouldn't have been able to tell you if I had the ability to blink my eyes, but I certainly could have told you that I didn't care. Mark seemed unaware of all this so I attempted to stare harder, letting him know I was trying to respond to him. The feeling I had was so distinct and menacing that I began to wonder if he was in trouble.

Can you hear me? Do you only know the thoughts that are about you or also the ones that are only meant for me? Maybe that's why I'm picking up an anxious distress, you're trapped in your own mind, screaming to be set free. You know I'm here, outside of you, but can't tell that I know you're in there screaming for me. That has to be it. Nothing else makes any sense. I thought at him as hard as I could.

Marisol suddenly burst forth from the balcony door startling both of us, though neither of us moved; I felt Mark's surprise for him, the very definition of vicarious. We did however finally come into our space and lock eyes, and for a brief moment, I felt an overwhelming and surprising rush of hatred for Mark. The feeling seized me so tightly that there was nothing else in the world more real than this new realization.

You're not trapped in there, you're fooling me, and keeping me distracted for some reason. And it's not a new behavior! What could the reason be?! What have I ever done to you?! Why have I been used and been subject to this treason of trust?! I must be the receiver and you're the transmitter, but I bet that can be reversed too.

Marisol was speaking Spanish very loudly and at a speed unnatural for even a native speaker. I watched Mark jolt out of his chair, breaking our connection, and face her, telling her to quiet down. He had the look of absolute terror on his face, and I noted this with a pleased curiosity, believing I was on the right path to discover a truth about Mark that was being revealed to me. *He isn't aware that I still have the telepathic link, the fool.*

Marisol turned and stormed back into the apartment, still speaking a mile a minute. She was pointing at the bedroom doors, the balcony door, the vaporizer on the table, the iPod and at Mark, but neither Mark nor I knew any Spanish. This didn't stop Mark from grabbing her by the arms and shaking her in a desperate attempt to calm her. I hung back, closed the door to the balcony, and observed the scene, noting every detail of their movements for the puzzle I was putting together in my mind.

Marisol calmed a bit, looked Mark straight in the face and repeated herself very slowly but still in Spanish. "[In Spanish] I said that I finally figured out the messages in the song I was playing, I had to do it 17 times but I got the message. My roommate will be coming home soon unexpectedly, and she will be very upset. We have to thank the iPod for this divine message and then act normal the rest of the night."

"I don't speak Spanish Mari, you'll have to tell me in English if you want me to understand." Mark replied with equal calm staring her hard in the face.

Marisol's face flashed with anger, "[In Spanish] What are you talking about? I'm speaking perfect English. Are you trying to play a joke on me, because it's not funny and this is very serious!" She shouted, shaking her arms free of his grip. She then stormed over her roommate's door, pointing her fingers and shouting, still unaware that she wasn't actually speaking in English.

Mark turned to me with a bewildered expression, "What the fuck is going on dude, she's lost it".

I struggled but forced my voice to work and "I don't know" was all I could muster, but I was in agreement that she may have lost it. I didn't want to blow my cover so I slowly got up, not breaking eye contact with Mark and moved towards him in what felt like a levitation, carrying my next words on the tip of my tongue, using all my strength to hold the words back but not lose them, projecting only their meaning through my eyes, and finally, when right in front of him, said, "I know."

"What?" Mark said sounding confused. I was obviously following two narratives at the same time, and in an effort to be concise I had answered to both of them in the most sincere, honest, and thorough way, one in the negative and one in the affirmative. I couldn't have been clearer honestly. Due to the telepathic link, Mark should know which reply answered which narrative. Asking 'what' just proved to me more that Mark was using and deceiving me.

Marisol stepped in-between us, almost severing the link "[In Spanish] Asa, Asa, my very best friend, you have to listen to me, snap out of your haze! The iPod told me what was going to happen! Don't you believe me? Please say that you do, I know it sounds crazy especially since you didn't hear it, but we are going to be found out shortly when she gets home, and there is no way I can stop her from ratting us out, and that would be really sad because I will be deported and the two of you would go to jail for drugs! I'm so scared right now!"

I listened to every word, attempting to understand her speaking in the same way as Mark's thoughts, but I got nothing from her and instead began to laugh and force more words, "Ok ok ok....... English."

Marisol scowled, huffed, and returned to her crouched position in front of the iPod and began playing the same song again at high tracking speed. "[In Spanish] You guys are stupid assholes; I really am getting messages here and you should listen to me. The iPod won't let me down, it never has in the past, it'll be kinder and more honest than you two! Maybe it'll tell me more if I keep listening."

"*Just dance. It'll be ok...*"

Mark and I looked at her briefly then looked back to one another, linking back up, "we need to calm her down. Let's try some alcohol" mark said as he walked over to the table, poured some drinks, and put on a pair of oversized ladies' sunglasses, "you tracers are giving me a headache" he said into the air.

You won't break out connection that easily, I'm all up in your head now. I thought at him. He set a glass of wine next to Marisol and handed one to me before picking up his own, "I'm so fucked up dude. Tell me, is she really not speaking English or am I just imagining it?"

I took a large swallow of the wine and looked back deeply into his eyes despite the lenses, *You're not imaging that, she's speaking Spanish, but that's not important; I know who you are and what you're up to now.* Surely if I thought it loud enough there was no way he wouldn't hear and understand it, but he demurred. We remained staring at one another for a moment, him remaining very still in an effort not give away anything and me with the intent that I would catch it once he did; we were actively ignoring each other while remaining completely present in the moment.

"Roommate! Home!" Marisol suddenly screamed the two words with an exasperated breath, removing her hand from the iPod just long enough get out the English words.

"Oh shit." Mark said as I thought it simultaneously.

I knew we were still linked you motherfucker.

There was lightning fast movement from both Mark and I to clear the tables of all the mess and drug paraphernalia. When Marisol noticed this she began laughing hysterically,

"[In Spanish] oh my god, what is happening?! I said the exactly same thing as I did before but this time, I said it to you in Spanish and you understood; the iPod was right again! When did you guys learn Spanish words?!"

"She managed some English words so it's not a total loss, but we're all too fucked up to be around sober people right now, we should just barricade into Mari's room and ride this out." Mark said with a slight shake in his voice. His heartbeat must have been up due to the fear of what I was discovering.

In our scramble to move the party to Marisol's bedroom, Mark was going on about how dark it was, and worrying that he was beginning to blackout, forgetting that he had put on sunglasses. In contrast, I was more lucid and aware of things than I had ever been in my whole life, and I decided not to remind him of the sunglasses as a form of revenge.

It was difficult to get Marisol and the iPod into the room because she believed that if she unplugged it then she would lose the ability to hear its messages. Mark easily overpowered her though, and carried her into the other room, and I was able to get the system set back up fairly quickly after locking the door to her room.

Marisol's bedroom was trashed. There were plates of moldy food under the bed, long black hair all over the bathroom, makeup all over the mirrors, and massive piles of dirty clothing in the corners. She had returned to the iPod and resumed her scrolling for new messages. The sensory overload tossed me into a debilitated state and I was immediately more jealous of Mark because he might be spared this stress due to the sunglasses.

This is too much, we need to clean this place if we're not planning on leaving, it's too much, don't you see it?

Mark didn't respond so I took the initiative to start kicking her clothes into more distinct piles. This broke Marisol's trance on the iPod as she stood up and got in my face.

"[In Spanish] Stop! What're you doing?! You're mixing up all my dirty clothes with clothes I've only tried on that're still clean!"

"Goddammit speak English!" Mark yelled.

"Shhhhhh" Marisol hissed, using her hands as a signal to lower the sounds. Thankfully 'shh' is the same in all languages. We all understood this and for a short moment the room became calmer due to the cohesive communication. I began to move the clothing more slowly as a result, to which Marisol stared up at me and repeated the 'shhhhh' sound every time I moved my foot. I stood still and she nodded approvingly while still hissing 'shhhhh'. Mark began to chuckle a bit, which made me begin to laugh a bit too.

Mark I'm not going to be laughed out of our connection and what I now understand is your long-standing manipulation of me. I thought at him.

"SHHHHHHHHHHHHHHHH" Marisol hissed louder, as if she could hear my thoughts too. I began laughing for real now and coupled with

Mark's snickering overcame Marisol's desire to be quiet and we all lost our wits.

I couldn't move. I just stood in the center of the room while Marisol laid across the foot of her bed and Mark sat on the floor under the window, all of us laughing. I wanted so badly to speak but I couldn't form words and when I attempted to think at them, I was derailed by the laughter. I'm not sure how long it went on but we must have heard that entire lady ga ga song 10 times on repeat before the laughing subsided.

Silence eventually descended for a time, and it seemed at first that we were coming down, but in that moment, I began to hear Mark's body movements again.

I can still hear you, are you going to persist in ignoring me? I see you looking at her, and I know you want her, but I'll step in and take her myself before I'll ever let you have her. Are you just my friend because I help you get your dick wet with strippers and we don't really know anyone else? How dare you charge me for something freely offered and at a time when saying 'no' would have been impolite. I dare you. I dare you to get up from the floor and touch her. Give me a reason to smash your skull!

"Mari, do you think it's safe to return to the living room? Surely if your roommate was going to show up, she would be here by now right?" Mark Asked.

[In English] "Oh I don't know, maybe, what time it even is? Can we all be calm and quiet at least? Asa?"

I can be calm, I have other ways to communicate, but I think Mark should leave. I thought sternly, taking note of the fact that Marisol speaking English again signaled that we were coming down.

"Back to English again? Finally. And, I can do that easily enough." Mark said.

Do what easily, be quiet or leave? Can you hear me or not?!

"I also think Asa should maybe sit down; he's making me nervous."

Fuck you, Mark, I will end you!

"Shhhhhhh, we're being too loud again. Asa, you should sit down." Marisol asserted.

Not until he's gone and you're mine. I'm not usually the type to give ultimatums but I can't continue otherwise.

"Hm, ok, stand if you like, I'll go see what's up, hold on." Marisol whispered, clearly answering to my ultimatum.

As she left the room Mark looked up at me with a frustration that was full of determination. "Why are you just standing there like that? Why do you keep staring? What are you so worried about?"

Like you don't know. I'm not going to let you have her, and I'm not going to let you use me anymore. I stared.

"Ok, well, I'm glad she has calmed down some though, what she was doing with the music and then all the shushing was really getting on my nerves, I could barely hold it together."

No excuse for ignoring me when I'm standing up for myself.

"She's looking crazy sexy tonight though, I bet if you wanted to you could have her." He smirked a little.

Oh, are you trying to persuade me with a bribe? Like you're doing me a favor by not going after her?

"If you wanted to that is. She acts virtuous but she isn't, I can guarantee you."

What is that supposed to mean? You think she's lying about her virginity? Like you would've had a chance anyway.

"What is she doing out there? I'll go check." Mark said and exited the room. I could hear voices and it seemed her roommate was definitely home. I was still having trouble moving and I couldn't make out the topic of conversation but I managed to force fall forward into Marisol's bed and in an instant, I passed out.

The dream I had was of a city built somewhere onto the side of a mountain slowly being eroded away by rain and mudslides. I stood on an opposite mountain and witnessed a hundred years of decay in an instant. I watched but couldn't understand why the citizens or the city itself made no efforts to save what they had built or put in place certain protections to go against the natural devastation. I watched the population rise and fall, the buildings expand and decay, the roads lengthen then disappear, and the color of life burn from vibrant to a flicker. Eventually the city was completely gone, swallowed up by the earth and there was hardly any trace that anything had been there in the first place. Just before I woke, I saw a group of men hiking through the valley looking up to where the city had been, and remarking on rumors that a once great culture thrived here but had been lost to time because of their lack of purpose, preparation, and ability to look beyond the pleasures of the perpetual now.

I woke up in my underwear, with Marisol dressed in pajamas, but wrapped cozily around me and I didn't know what to think. I laid still for a moment reflecting on my dream, but was a bit distracted due to her large breast pressed up against me and the heat shared by our bodies.

"What all happened that I don't remember? Where was Mark? What time was it? Where are my clothes?

Marisol woke to my stirring and laughed at my expression of confusion.

"Don't worry friend, we didn't sleep together or anything like that, but I did try to make sure you were comfortable, I hope you don't mind."

"I don't mind really, though I don't think I would have been opposed to anything happening between us last night."

"Noooo I can't come between two friends like that, it wouldn't be right."

"Wait, what? You mean you and Mark?

"Yeah, of course, he's so alpha, we fooled around a couple times but he always wants to go too far too fast and I feel bad after. Oh, please don't tell him I told you! I promised not to mention it."

I was surprised at the brazen honesty, but also hurt. The hurt was delayed though because intuitively I already knew it. I had known it, but didn't want to see it. I laid silently for a moment, letting all the information come to fruition. My trip the night before had been illuminating, and I had a new sense of clarity on things. "Whatever, it's fine, I can't be his friend anymore after the conversation we had last night, if he even remembers it. I don't care."

"Oh, really? What did you talk about? And when? I don't understand, it wasn't because of me was it?"

"Yes and no, it's hard to explain. All the same, you also don't have to worry about coming between us now either."

"Oh nooo, I still couldn't do it, you're too good of a friend, and I don't want to ruin that. I only have a few friends and I want to keep you just the way you are."

This is a waste of my time. I thought suddenly and unexpectedly. I felt an overwhelming sense of confidence and impatience at the same time.

"Where is Mark by the way?"

"Oh, haha, he and my roommate hit it off and he stayed with her. She was so drunk."

I laid there in a position, and with a person I had wanted for a long time and almost couldn't' believe that as close as I was, though being rejected, I didn't really care. I couldn't believe my lack of feeling. I was numb and I felt strangely finished with all that I had been in the past. I wasn't getting anything I wanted out of life. My lifestyle wasn't fulfilling and it was growing more and more hurtful as time went on. I had no savings, no job in my intended career, no good female prospects, ignored emotional issues, and friendships based purely on the pursuit of physical pleasure.

I was a passive orbiter to all things, just a satellite to more substantial entities with more power and influence. Many will live and die in this state of affairs without thinking anything about it and in a way that is less tragic than knowing and doing nothing. Ignorance may be excused but cowardice can never be forgiven. My dream was now making complete sense to me.

"I see. Ok, I'm out. You have my number if you ever want to take me seriously."

"What do you mean?!"

I got up and dressed without responding. She looked at me questioningly, confused, and holding back some tears. I pretended not to notice as I patted my pockets, checking to ensure I had all my things. She buried her face in her hands as I walked out of the room. The last thing I heard was the bedroom door hitting the wall a little too hard.

Just A Little Routine Obsession

Friday:

4:00am – The battery powered analog alarm clock goes off with a deafening ring. Reach over and flip the switch to the off position. Press button on the back to shine a light on the hands. Ensure the time is right. It is.

4:01am – Sit up on the edge of the bed. Complete darkness. Open the floor to ceiling blackout curtains. Take note of the weather; dry, no need for a raincoat today. Walk to living room and open an identical set of curtains.

4:03am – Walk to the kitchen, hit the lights, start stove burner under the pre-poured pot of 8oz of water and pull out prepped glass food container, a jar of sauerkraut, and an avocado from the refrigerator.

4:05am – Open first 1/3 gallon bottle of water. Drink up to half.

4:06am – Fill steam grate with contents of prepped container. 4oz of griddle cooked organic beef, 1oz of spinach, 3oz of cut beets, 3oz of broccoli, 3oz of brussel sprouts, and 3oz of cauliflower.

4:09am –Fork 1oz of sauerkraut into the empty glass container. Cut the avocado in half, spoon one half into the container and store the second half. Pour in some olive oil.

4:11am – Fill and pack two 1/3 gallon stainless steel prefilled bottles of filtered water into backpack sleeves.

4:14am – Walk to laundry room, pull out gym shorts, shirt, and towel from dryer, and place into gym bag, checking for an extra pair of socks and underwear. Carry bag to front door.

4:16am – Continue back to bedroom, make bed, choose days clothing from closet and lay them out in the living room by the door.

4:19am – Dress out into running clothes, and run 1 mile around the apartment complex (8.5 minutes); not bad.

4:30am – Head to toilet and empty the bowls. Kick underwear to corner.

4:35am – One round of pushups to failure (PR of 75) followed by bicycle sit-ups to failure (PR of 50 each side). Getting better.

4:40am – Stand tall in front of bed, extend arms, close eyes, and spin clockwise chanting personal mantra three times. Repeat counterclockwise. Finish the spin in prayer pose, then one sun salutation, warrior 1, warrior 2, triangle pose, and reverse warrior on the clockwise side. Repeat on counterclockwise side. Kneel and say the Lord's Prayer aloud.

4:45am – Turn on shower, listen to ensure water is moving smoothly through vitamin C filter. Check back, chest, shoulders, ass, and face for pimples or blemishes.

4:47am – Step into shower, adjust water to a warm steam, and soak entire body.

4:49am – Step out of the water, squeeze some homemade baking soda shampoo into the hands and scrub hair and beard thoroughly. Switch spray of detachable showerhead to jet and rinse the steam off the hanging mirror. Re-holster the showerhead, and face the nozzle toward the curtain. Locate razor, run it across the forearm backwards to true the blade. Shave neck and cheek stubble, using the mirror to ensuring proper lines. Rinse the razor.

4:55am – Switch nozzle back to shower and rinse hair and beard until free of soap. Squeeze some homemade apple cider vinegar conditioner into hair, and rub into beard.

4:57am – Squeeze non-GMO store bought body soap onto chest and rub into all nooks and crannies of body.

4:59am – Pull showerhead out of holster and rinse everything off. Re-holster and rinse vinegar out of hair.

5:00am – Face wall with water streaming down the top of the head and face. Turn the shower nozzle all the way cold and begin to focus on breathing. Tilt head in all directions ensuring water touches every part. Turn around to get the back and then the front again. Turn water off.

5:05am – Grab closest towel, dry off face, hair, chest, right leg, step out of tub. Left leg, step out of tub. Drag towel down back, wrap around waist and secure. Close shower curtain and move far, driest towel to closer position before opening the door to let out steam. Take hand towel and clear mirror.

5:07am – Apply pomade to hair and comb a straight, smooth part. Apply a dab of coconut oil into beard and on any dry skin patches. Remove towel and dry once more then hang up in the far position.

5:11am – Head to living room, put on underwear, wake up computer. Check phone, no messages. Check the weather temperature. Sunny, 57 now with a high of 77 later. No need for a jacket at all.

5:13am – Computer is on. Open browser, make claims on cryptocurrency faucets at five sites switching between phone and desktop using the same sites with different logins. See if any interesting jobs are posted. None.

5:17am – Walk to kitchen, food is steamed. Spoon out tray into empty container. Coffee maker turns on.

5:18am – Rinse out tray and pot, and wipe down counter.

5:20am – Pull out supplement container and take first set. 1 allergy pill, 1 lions mane, 1 B-12 Folate, 1 Turmeric, 1 Long Jack, 1 Vitamin K-D3, 1 Ashwagandha, 1 MSM, and 1 DHEA using the remainder of the first 1/3 gallon of bottled water. Set bottle in sink and place supplement container.

5:22am – Open refrigerator and make a mental note of its contents.

5:24am - Head to bathroom to floss and brush teeth, finishing with tongue scrapper. Retrieve dirty underwear and walk to laundry room. Toss it into washer.

5:27am – Finish dressing with pants and shirt, pull out wallet, utility knife, work badges, watch, and pistol from drawer. Lace up boots.

5:29am – Put computer to sleep.

5:30am – Strap on watch, work badge, pocket the wallet, and knife, slide pistol into belt.

5:33am – Pour coffee, turn off machine, dump grounds, place coffee cup next to bags at front door, and turn off remaining lights.

5:35am – Unlock and open door. Remotely unlock car from door. Shoulder gym bag, pick up backpack, retrieve coffee, and lock door back.

5:37am – Gym bag and backpack in the back seat, gun in the door panel, coffee in the cup holder, phone and iPod on magnet mounts, seatbelt and lights on.

5:41am – Plug in 2006 iPod with no wifi ability and begin 10 minute positive affirmation file created with own voice and enough time in-between each statement for repeating it aloud. "*I am powerful*" "I am powerful"

5:43am – Take the usual route, which is half a mile and 30 seconds faster than the next best alternative. Continue repeating affirmations. "*Beautiful women are drawn to me*" "Beautiful women are drawn to me"

5:46am – Hit the interstate, ease into the left lane, reach 80mph. Continue repeating affirmations. "*I am successful and attract a high income*" "I am successful and attract a high income"

5:56am – Exit interstate toward office building, staying in the lines around the sharp 180-degree turn at 50mph. Finish affirmations "*I am a King*" "I am a King". Shut off radio. Continue driving in silence.

5:59am – Back into the odd space of the parking lot surrounded by vegetation islands close to the front door. Check emails on phone. Just newsletters. I'll read later. Browse twitter.

6:00am – Building manager arrives. Exit car, grab coffee, shoulder backpack, enter building, and take stairs three flights to the top floor.

6:07am – Arrive at desk, unpack food, store wallet and keys, turn on computer and pour first cup of coffee from travel cup to ceramic mug.

6:09am – Go into email spam folder and unsubscribe where able then delete all.

6:11am – View calendar. No holidays or events this weekend.

6:12am – View next week's bills. Nothing due next week, but the following Monday is the first so need to make sure there is enough money for rent. Make note to print out all statements to update budget for the month.

6:13am – Open Amazon, Craigslist, and eBay; all items for sale still in strong position.

6:14am – View excel file 'life tracker' access sheet for any potential password changes. None scheduled. Add some accounts to the 'delete later' column noticed from spam folder.

6:15am – Pull up iCloud desktop notepad entry 'fitness'. Open excel file 'life tracker', navigate to the fitness sheet. Record yesterday's leg workout numbers. Today is shoulders and grocery day.

6:16am – Navigate to notepad entry for 'grocery' and 'life tracker' sheet for grocery and plan out what needs to be bought from memory of the fridge this morning.

6:20am – Check that notepad updated on phone.

6:21am – Close all personal windows and open up work related documents. Put on headphones with instrumental synthwave music, phone on 'do not disturb'. Get to work.

8:00am – Alarm goes off. Finish off remaining coffee, use bathroom, and prep 8oz of hot lemon ginger tea. Check phone, no messages.

8:25am – Have cup of lemon ginger tea.

8:30am – Headphones in, back to work.

11:00am – Alarm goes off for Lunch. Finish off remaining tea, use bathroom, and open up second 1/3 gallon bottle of water. Check phone, no messages.

11:15am – Eat prepped meal.

11:25am – Take walk around the parking lot in the sun.

11:35am – Use bathroom, prep second cup of lemon ginger tea, headphones in, and head back to work.

2:00pm – Alarm goes off, use the bathroom, and finish second cup of tea. Check phone, no messages.

2:12pm – Clean up desk, dishes, and save all work done during the day. Sign timecard, take one scoop of creatine monohydrate, and finish off second 1/3 gallon bottle of water. Remove 'do not disturb' status from phone, and pack up bag.

2:15pm – Use bathroom and head to car. Remove third 1/3 gallon bottle of water from bag and transfer to gym bag. Remove watch, knife, wallet, and badges, place them in backpack.

2:20pm – Drive to gym, dress out, and empty bowls again.

2:30pm – Stretch out and cardio.

2:45pm – Weight training.

3:30pm – Abs

3:45pm – Sauna, steam, jacuzzi, and cold rinse. Dress, and head out.

4:00pm – Drive to grocery store. Enjoy old new wave music with the windows down.

4:20pm – Produce section, meat section, dry goods section, and supplement section with all items on list located. Check phone, no messages.

4:45pm – Drive home with more music, sun, and wind.

4:50pm – Arrive home, have all groceries in the apartment in one trip. All groceries in cabinets, refrigerator, and freezer.

5:00pm – Use bathroom, check phone, no messages.

5:06pm – Set up pot and steam tray, fill with prepped dinner container with 8oz chicken thigh, 1oz of spinach, 3oz of cut beets, 3oz of broccoli, 3oz of brussel sprouts, and 3oz of cauliflower.

5:15pm – Take evening supplements of 2 Fish Oil, 1 Glycine, 1 Zinc, 1 Calcium, and 1 Magnesium. Wash down with 1oz of Apple Cider Vinegar and rest of third 1/3 gallon bottle of water.

5:20pm – Walk to mailbox and lap around apartment complex.

5:35pm – Food is steamed. Transfer to bowl with olive oil, second half of previously cut avocado, 1oz of sauerkraut, season with Himalayan salt, pepper, garlic, and turmeric. Switch on computer, navigate to YouTube and que up videos on health, fitness, and politics. Eat dinner

5:40pm – Fill dishwasher with all remaining dirty dishes. Turn on dishwasher. Separate laundry and start first load of socks, underwear, towels, and workout clothing.

5:50pm – Pull out large pot, fill ½ the way with water, and place in 6 8oz chicken thighs. Add in salt, pepper, garlic, and coconut oil. Turn on stovetop.

5:53pm – Unwrap beef and portion out into 6 4oz portions using analog scale. Place them all on a plate and set aside.

6:08pm - Lay out 12 medium sized glass containers with tops off next to cutting board. Pull down strainer. Put all produce in sink for rinsing.

6:15pm – Rinse off all produce.

6:21pm – Chicken is finished. Turn off burner and allow to sit and cool.

6:23pm – Cube cut beets and portion into 12 containers.

6:37pm – Dump chicken water and portion cooked thighs into 6 of the containers.

6:41pm – Place griddle across stove eyes, cover with coconut oil, and lay out beef portions. Turn stove to medium heat.

6:43pm – Move clothes from washer to dryer and replace with shirts and pants. Start machines.

6:50pm – Portion out 1oz of spinach into containers. Flip beef portions over. Sprinkle on pepper and garlic.

7:00pm – Portion 3oz of broccoli and 3oz of brussel sprouts into containers. Flip beef portions again.

7:08pm – Turn off stove and move beef portions to the second 6 containers.

7:20pm – Move griddle to other end of stove for cooling. Wipe off excess with a damp towel and soak up any splattered grease.

7:28pm – Chop up cauliflower, portion 3oz each into the containers, and cap them off. Store any excess into a large container and place all containers into the refrigerator.

7:35pm – Dishwasher is finished, unload, and clean up all dishes and counters, turn off computer, transfer clothes from dryer to hamper and washer to dryer.

7:45pm – Fill three 1/3 gallon bottles with filtered water and set aside.

7:58pm – Strip bed of sheets and blankets and place into the washing machine. Start machines.

8:00pm – Turn on projector in living room, close curtains, and select a film to watch. Check phone, no messages.

8:05pm – Sit on couch with hamper and fold first load of laundry with film playing on wall.

8:30pm – Put up folded clothes, retrieve pipe, lighter, and ashtray from cabinet. Relax with a smoke on the couch.

9:05pm – Transfer second load of laundry to hamper and bedding to dryer. Start machine and carry clothes back to couch for folding.

9:30pm – Put up folded clothes, use bathroom, check phone, no messages. Resume smoking pipe and watching film.

9:58pm – Movie is over. Turn off projector and speakers, put away pipe, and ashtray, pull out tomorrows supplement container, and set next to bottles of water.

10:05pm – Transfer bedding to hamper and carry to bedroom. Make up bed with clean sheets.

10:10pm – Brush teeth, check body for pimples, blemishes, or scrapes.

10:15pm – Get into bed, set battery powered analog alarm clock to 4 am. Read self-improvement passages until sleepy.

"Wish I could meet someone to talk to."

Project the Possession

The ice storm had made all the roads completely unusable. The southeast is woefully unprepared and inexperienced with driving in snow and ice, so the only thing to be done is nothing at all. It wasn't for lack of intelligence, as many northerners liked to parrot, but just the simple fact that inexperience and lack of exposure fostered a deficiency; how many native Bostonians would be able to keep calm during a tornado, after all?

Max thought about such things when he went out driving on his neighborhood street to see if the hill leading down and out of the subdivision was thawed, each time being forced back home. He was stuck and there was no telling how long. Thankfully, he had electricity, cell service, a fridge full of food, and plenty of alcohol.

Max texted Sarah periodically throughout the day, sharing memes, telling jokes, attempting to flirt, and trying to make plans to get together once the ice melted. His text game was usually on point, but Sarah was infrequent and long between her replies, all of which were brief and vaguely dismissive, and Max would grow insecure that he was appearing desperate. He would then try to beat her at her own game by not responding quickly. She always won. This just created an exhausting drawn out exchange that didn't qualify as a conversation at all, and he wondered why she would still reach out.

Max passed the time watching TV, playing Xbox, and lying in bed with his laptop. No matter what he did though, he would obsessively look over at his phone every few seconds waiting on Sarah's replies. He laughed at himself for how absurd he was being, as if he hadn't had plenty of women or played the game before. All the same, he couldn't seem to control his eyes repeatedly checking for alerts; she wasn't even that interesting, he thought. He found he didn't look at it as much if he turned the screen off. Spurred on by boredom though, he kept it open playing games and checking Facebook, eventually finding himself refreshing her page for the potential of new statuses or comment threads. Nothing.

He began to wonder if maybe her part of town didn't have much ice, and she was therefore able to go out and about. She claimed she was just at home with her mom watching movies, which seemed weird as Sarah often spoke of how she hated her mom and would typically use any reason to ignore her. She also complained of sitting still for long periods and always had her phone next to her. Max knew he was being ignored but cast it off as evidence of deeper interest at the most and legitimate preoccupation at the least. The fantasy of her was growing sweeter despite his efforts to dispel it.

Around 10pm, he saw an update on Treys Facebook saying, "we out here doing it live! Ice storm be damned!", and Max wondered darkly if maybe he was with Sarah. Tray had so many girls around him these days, but he was discreet if nothing else. Trey also hadn't returned Max's texts for almost 3 months. Fat chance he would start now, especially for an inquiry about who he was spending time with. Why did he assume he was with Sarah? The possibilities of what's happening out in the world have no limits and Max could easily connect the dots separated by huge gaps. This way of thinking was part of what made him so charming to women in the first place.

Max sighed. It was 2am and he felt numb. He put his phone away, got in bed, opened his laptop, popped in his ear buds, and spent the next couple of hours watching porn before falling asleep.

Max awoke at 1pm. His mouth hot and dry. His laptop was still open, cycling through videos on an endless loop, his earbuds having popped out as he finished himself off hours before. He didn't feel rested at all, and his sheets were damp as if he had peed in the night, but it was just the sweat generated from his body. His laptop running to full capacity on his stomach for many hours, heating him up just added to the puddle. The night of sweating mixed with the cold on the sheets created a swampy feel and a putrid, awful smell generated because of the cold humidity. He was deathly thirsty, and mused darkly that he had been in danger of electrocution.

He took a moment to absorb his situation and felt a moment of deep shame but that was easily dismissed as it had been so many times before. He began to wonder though if the blue-lit screen of sex playing all night had uploaded something weird into his dreams. All sorts of weird videos were pushed on him through the "you may also like" algorithms and he didn't know why. He wasn't into old, fat, married, or blood related women but the ads and suggestions sure wanted him to be. So be it, he thought, and quickly dressed to go outside and check the ice. Solid as a rock.

He pulled up his phone to see a message from Sarah, "This ice storm is insane! Hope you're staying warm!" :::Kiss with heart emoji:::

She said nothing about getting together later in the week. Max assumed she was just keeping him on a long line for her amusement. He hated her for an instant and then put on a movie to pass the time. Then another before taking a nap. There was nothing else to do.

As evening rolled around Max indulged in the liquor he had in the house. He sent over two hundred messages to women on OKCupid, received 3 boring replies, and watched a dozen episodes of a TV show he had no interest in. Max disliked regular TV but would let anything play in the background if he had nothing else to do. He suddenly realized he hadn't showered all day but just laughed it off. If it was possible to degrade himself any further based on what he had at his disposal he couldn't think of it, and that was only for lacking company and supplies. He took to his phone and swiped through tinder till it cut him off. No matches. He was growing restless.

He began to pace around, irritated that he wasn't getting any quality replies online. He ultimately took it up a notch and began to troll craigslist, answering all the personal ads just to get some semblance of a response. He didn't care if it was spam, a bot, or even some old dude pretending to be a girl. His excitement came out of the new message alert on his phone. The dopamine hit of reward. The desire to know that someone wanted to get in touch with him was fulfilled, regardless of the reason.

This momentary fragment of pleasure sent a jolt straight to the brain. The more ads he answered the more responses he received; he had no intention or capability of meeting anyone anyway. The ice prevented him for one, but in the end, none of them were Sarah. *What was she up to and why hadn't she gotten back to me all day long?* he thought, fighting the urge not to show his desperation by texting her again.

The majority of the replies he received were clearly automated and the rest were never from any human being of substance. Kind of like real life, he mused. At least this way he could pretend the rejection wasn't real. He could just continue generating the reward for hours on end. He was a jingle junkie. An alert addict.

When his energy was almost shot and his buzz was just about to pass over into full on drunkenness, he got back in bed with his laptop and navigated to the live nude cam sites. He knew his money was good enough to get some kind of attention, fleeting though it was. Maybe I'll find another sweet girl in Southeast Asia that favors me over the others and eventually gives me private shows for free, he thought with a smirk. This happened often and he didn't question what it was about him that was naturally magnetic to women in this part of the world, he just indulged. They said it was because of his large nose.

These sites had the interface down to a science and it sucked in many who dared to use it. There were literally thousands of women sitting on their web cams all around the world. They just sat and waited for men to come chat and request sexual behavior for monetary tips. The front page would be a graphic mosaic of thumbnails, each of a particular girl that moved a bit when your mouse hovered over it, just enough to entice you. You could open many tabs on your browser, each with a different girl and even get alerts when your favorite model signed in. It was like LinkedIn but with tits and a surprisingly fast bank withdrawal system.

Max's habit would be to open up 15-20 tabs, select the best 6-9, minimize them into small windows, and then arrange them on screen so he could see them all at once. He would constantly shift his eyes in every direction trying to catch them all as he brought himself to orgasm, like a perverse version of EMDR. He called it porno Pokémon and it never took very long to climax. The rapid change of focus every couple of seconds ended up being a part of the fun. *On which one will my eyes lock, when the muscles seize up and cock becomes one with sock*, he mused. If he really liked one of the girls, he would close all the others and edge himself back and forth until she got dirty enough for free. They often did.

Tonight was no different, except that one girl caught his attention and he couldn't figure out what it was about her. The alcohol had hit him and one eye started to close the longer he tried to maintain his erection. Blood flow is a funny thing.

She was ranked highly and had a full room. She stood out from the rest to more men than just Max. He pondered her for a moment. Good enough for tonight, he thought, and removed the sock, revived his mediocre erection to a point where it was just enough to feel a sensation. He dribbled out onto the sheets, rolled over into his mess and fell asleep.

2:30 pm. Max wakes up. His laptop was still on. Again. Thankfully, no loop running this time, just a nude girl, feet up on her

71

desk, face hidden, and reading the Tom Robbins novel *Still Life, with Woodpecker*.

That book is poetically fitting, thought Max, and just took in the sight. The chill in the air made him snuggle into the blanket and he felt a pleasant peace nested in his bed, looking at this girl casually reading.

This went on for many minutes and he wondered if she had been up all night and morning camming. There were still a couple of hundred people in the room but no one was really chatting. It was as if they were all just taking it in as well. He was enthralled and regarded with joy the pleasant feeling he was allowing to envelop him. Suddenly, the girl's phone went off on her desk, startling her out of her book and him out of his trance. *That was cute. We just shared a moment,* Max thought with affection. He chuckled. He'd have to favorite her and check back later on. He had a killer hangover.

No positive change in the road conditions but instead they had gotten worse. *Whatever,* Max thought, *I need to clean the place up anyway, it stinks.*

Max checked his phone to find some messages from Sarah and was suddenly very excited:

11:34am "In these stolen moments, the world is mine, there's nobody here, just us together."

11:36am "what're you up to right now?"

Is she trying to write poetry or quoting song lyrics, he wondered. He had a love hate reaction to her often-cryptic way of infrequent messaging.

He responded with a gif of a man making 'come hither' eyes. "Nothing much, :::wink face emoji::: surviving the ice and riding the couch at home. What're you up to?"

He also noticed over 100 email replies from his craigslist perusal session, but since it was daytime and he was no longer fiending he deleted them all without reading. No more OKCupid messages though, and no new tinder matches; what a joke of an industry.

Max gathered up all his dirty clothes for the wash, filled the dishwasher, wiped the counters, swept all the floors, and had a hot shower. He was finally feeling the end of the hangover and was feeling an energy rush when he realized he forgot to clean his dirty sheets. Ironically the most disgusting thing in the apartment by now. He'd get to it soon but he needed to eat first.

As he sat eating and watching the weather forecast, he checked his phone again. Sarah hadn't replied to his last texts and he sighed, thinking that he shouldn't have sent the meme.

His mind wandered to the cam girl he found so charming. What was it about her that had simultaneously provoked all his focus and relaxed him? Maybe he just liked the quiet nature she projected or how sincere her amusement was when she was startled by her phone. Either way he was anxious to watch her again and try to interact. He had nothing to do at the moment, and even though he had convinced himself that he wanted to read, he really didn't care to. He just wanted to see if she was online. It may be a fun indulgence to pass the time and distract me from waiting on Sarah, *I win at each turn*, he thought slyly. His laptop was still on his bed and in his excitement, he dove in without even removing his shoes. Clean sheets be damned.

She was online. "Yeeesssssss" Max said aloud, his limp dick already being massaged in his hand.

She was sitting at a table typing replies to the other room members. There were approximately 900 right now, but all you could see was the bottom of her breast and her neck due to how she had the camera positioned. He didn't care, her breasts were just what he liked, and she had good posture, which he appreciated. There was a lightness to her movements and he couldn't help but attach the idea of innocence to her despite the non-innocent nature of her current behavior. *Mysterious*, he thought with an amused feeling vibrating through him. He began to bob his head to her electro music. He didn't really require much of her image and the feeling it produced to become fully erect. He was done in no time. He drifted off in post dopamine sleep.

Max awoke suddenly to loud music coming from his laptop. It was 10am and his new girl was rocking out to some 80's new wave. *I think I'm in love*, he thought.

This time the camera was beneath the desk pointed up so you could view her entire under carriage as she played with herself. Max was once again ready in an instant to use her image for himself, and took note that she groomed herself but didn't shave bald as so many of the others. Good, he thought, he always wondered why that was a thing. It was too pedo for him, and he hated how women always wanted to look younger but get angry when men like younger women.

He edged himself for a while, keeping pace with her as if they were dependent on one another. He noticed that he was getting to the point in his stimulus response that he was longer between orgasm sessions, yet shorter for the time it took to finish once hard; the opposite of the ideal. *Could it be the porn*, he thought briefly. He scrubbed these thoughts and found he was timing his ejaculation just in sync with hers on screen. These were the best cam moments for him. He was in ecstasy.

3:45pm Max wakes up. His fixation on the new cam girl was now so pronounced that he left her page up while he was doing other stuff, carrying his lap top around the house. He began creating a sense of consistency that made him feel lonely but involved simultaneously. Most of the time he would mute it, though it wasn't needed due to her typically quiet behavior. It was nice to have something to look over at while playing games.

He began to notice that this girl never showed her face. She had no distinguishing marks or tattoos, barely spoke at length, and never revealed any personal information. She was nothing but a nude female using her body to visually please a thousand men at a time. This is why he signed up though, and to that end, she was just like all the others. The difference was this one grabbed hold of him in a place deeper down than his groin. Mysteriously fanning the flame of his buried desires for companionship.

He wasn't the only one either. He had quickly become part of a group of regulars who would share jokes or take shots at one another from time to time for fun. All agreed that they were taken in by her in a deep and relaxing manner. She never acknowledged this conversation topic past typing "thank you!" or some form of passive compliment meant to endear the men further. She was a professional after all.

Max pondered the fixation further and noticed it wasn't due to anything particularly aesthetic about her, but instead her ultimate anonymity. She was plain and nondescript enough that anyone watching could project onto her any woman they wanted, provided the desired projection was close enough to match her in size and race.

Max and his compatriots joined the ranks of other random men for hours on end using her as a virtual lint trap for projecting their ultimate female fantasy. All she had to do was be available, lounge seductively, answer the occasional flirty question, listen to music, and masturbate as the money and attention just poured in. The fact that she seemed to spend all day long here with several thousand sets of eyes on her, vying for her attention and giving her money was a testament to the dark depths of our culture. *Women have so much more power than they know or admit*, thought Max

Granted, this was why the cam industry was so popular in the first place. Whereas many models were either overflowing with a personality that the viewer had to accept first before he could enjoy the visual or they were an unemotional, unengaging face pasted on awkward bodies that reeked of possible sex slavery, this one though displayed a low vibration of paradox.

She exhibited forms of the traditional feminine traits of modesty, innocence, agreeableness, and cleanliness, but everything about the behavior in this context was exhibitionist, calculated, and dirty. *How can she do this while still embodying those traits? She's either deeply misguided or a diabolical psychopath,* Max thought, feeling a sense of angst brewing at not being able to get more from the interaction, his idea of femininity unable to embrace the paradoxical existence.

She flirted, sang, laughed with her whole body, and was an engaged performer, but remained in an in-between accessible and unreal. The regulars were likely all similar types of men in real life and they likely would all be very disappointed if they met the model face to face. Here in the virtual world though they could make her into anything they wanted. They would keep coming back for more. She had capitalized on the demand from men for more femininity by creating an abstract template of traditional fantasy, and the men paid her handsomely for it.

Objectively, the room was a nihilistic mass of idolatry to the flesh. They had no idea how finely they skirted the line between casual worship and obsession. All their reserved energy and diluted spiritual substance could have easily been amassed into a brutal crusade of virtue if only they had the motivation. Cults are built on much less.

Unattainable and ultimately disposable, their idol would never allow them to realize their potential because then they wouldn't need her. The longer they remained, the longer they were barred from all chance of ever going beyond their chemical desires. In fact, the more they indulged the harder it was to break away. They never seemed to mind and never moved on to something new. They were blind to the avenues towards transcendence.

Naturally, Max projected Sarah on the screen. He saw so much of her in the model that hour after hour, wrapped in his sweaty blanket, underwear tucked tightly under his balls, he would begin to wonder if in fact it really was her. He never asked Sarah directly if she was into camming, but it wasn't much of a stretch to imagine she was into it in principle if not in practice. It would certainly explain how she always had money but never seemed to work.

He oscillated back and forth in his mind about it being her or not being her. He wanted her so badly that he would tell himself that his desperation was getting the best of him and that the chances of finding her on a website were slim. He could just as easily convince himself that it was her and this was how the universe worked, constantly giving you what you want in a way that you don't want it.

I should bring this up to Sarah. At the very least, she'd be amused at the thought of my seeing her when she wasn't there. Maybe later on, for now just one more go round online. She's got really cute underwear on now, he thought as he let himself be engulfed by the images, stimulated by his warm body catching chills from the air as he got off, and twisted out from under his blanket.

Max woke up slowly. He couldn't see the clock. He must have knocked it off the table in the night. A while back, he had gotten a battery powered analog clock because he didn't like having electronics in the bedroom. The irony of the past few days was not lost on him. It was dark out so he assumed he must have slept through the whole day. Time had gotten away from him so quickly lately that whatever the clock read was irrelevant anyway.

His mind returned to the question of Sarah being his favorite cam model. He didn't' have the guts to bring up the topic of cam sex with Sarah directly. So, in efforts to ease his anxiety he broke his resistance and began to text Sarah while watching the model at the same time. He wanted to see if maybe the model looked at her phone or sent a text in sync with his attempts.

Conveniently, Sarah never text back and the model never looked at her phone when Max sent a text, but this did nothing to disprove it either. He then attempted to inquire about the model in ways that would give him clues to her more personal likes and dislikes in a ruse to draw a parallel to Sarah and then prove his suspicions correct.

The model didn't respond to him much after this. In his deep neurotic hole, he was now incapable of having small talk let alone flirting effectively. He would bust out of the gate with deep and weirdly cryptic questions that earned him plenty of mockery from other guys in the room. He didn't care.

Eventually this questioning behavior came off as too creepy to the model, and he was banned from conversation. It made more sense for her to join the other guys than to take him seriously. He was still able to watch and give money of course and he did so in feeble attempts to win back her favor, to no avail. This treatment felt a lot like his many interactions with the actual Sarah, competing with someone he deep down believed to be smarter and of higher status than himself. He felt strangely at home in this behavior despite its negative character. Being able to watch the model was more that he had ever gotten from Sarah so he rationalized that he was getting the best he could given the circumstances.

All this self-analysis had suddenly pulled him away from the chat room and he suddenly came back into his own body, *God these sheets smell bad. What has it been? Four nights of this? This ice needs to get gone so I can distract myself outside of this house.*

He lay still for a moment, becoming annoyed with how easy it was for him to become possessed with the thought of a girl, especially one he had never even seen naked. Then he shook his head in embarrassment as he realized he had become equally fixated on one whom he had only ever seen naked. If he had more from Sarah, he may not have been taken in by the image of the model as easily. If he could go out and socialize, he wouldn't be in the position in the first place.

Max sighed and looked around his dark bedroom. He exited the cam site and resorted to trolling craigslist the rest of the evening in a weak effort to move on from his overt rejection in the model's room. The best he got was a very obese and ugly older woman that kept sending him pictures of herself nude and bent over from behind. He stared at them and tried his best to become aroused until he finally became so disgusted that he closed his laptop for the first time since he opened it days ago. He went outside in his underwear and just stood still. He needed to feel something different. He didn't come back inside until his feet burned from the layer of frost on his balcony.

According to the TV, Max was finally able to leave his neighborhood safely. The city was brimming with activity and it appeared some of the other cars in his lot had left. He arose from the stink of his bed to answer his ringing phone.

"Hey! Are you still alive over there?" Sarah said with a giggle.

"Yeah, excited to get out of here. Wanna grab some food?"

"Nah I can't right now, I have some other plans. I really want to head out to my family's cabin tomorrow and I need a ride. You interested?"

"Yes of course! I would love to!" He said too easily and immediately regretted his tone.

"Great! I've been in an awful head space the last couple of days and I need to get out of town with good company. Pick me up at 7 tomorrow morning?"

"I can do that no problem. Is it just us?"

"Of course, sweetie! We don't spend enough time together."

Max hung up feeling full with excitement and stars in his eyes. It was as if he had been given access to a well of water after wandering in a desert. He wanted her attention and he got it. Finally. It was enough to buoy him all the rest of the morning.

Later in the evening, as he was packing for the trip, he suddenly realized that the cam model was offline for the first time since he had first seen her. *Shit, could it really be Sarah*, he thought. He shook his head to get rid of the poisonous thoughts. He knew he wouldn't be able to resist bringing the topic up with her and began plotting the best way to do it so as not to ruin the trip.

"Don't ruin this. Don't ruin this. Don't ruin this. Don't ruin this", he said to himself over and over again, almost chanting. It was the only way he knew to calm his nerves without sexual activity. He couldn't handle the idea that the girl he wanted could be camming and even felt like a hypocrite for indulging so easily in viewing it despite his opinion of those who did it. He set his alarm and forced himself to sleep.

Max woke up at six, groggy due to his unleveled sleep schedule. He instantly remembered he hadn't cleaned his sheets and wanted to make sure he at least stripped the bed before he left.

After a shower, he got a text from Sarah, "Hey, I need to cancel our trip. I forgot I have some important things to take care of. I'm sorry to let you down sweetie. :::kiss emoji::: I hope you understand and hope we can get together again soon!"

His heart sank. He hated himself. He gagged at the realization of being played for such a fool. As he sat and stewed in the emotions, stiff with pain, spinning in anger, he realized that he wanted her to change her mind again. He still wanted to go on the trip. Despite all, he still wanted to give her all his attention and affection. He would still allow her to give him relief from his suffering. He felt shame at his undesirability, and despair in his neediness. He had no direction out of this pit, and no inspiration or motivation to discover the existence of such a direction. All that existed was burning acid reflux and Sarah's absence. All he craved was the dissolvable foaming relief her company could provide.

Numb, he got back into his filthy bed. He pulled down his pants around his ankles, switched on his laptop, and found the mystery girl typing away to the room. *Thank god*, he thought, *I need this*.

As she began playing with herself, he followed in kind, and slowly, as his eyes glazed over, he started to forget.

Auto Asphyxiac Agitation

West End is a congested, and at times difficult stretch of road. It has scantly used street parking, is crisscrossed by one ways with questionable signage, switches wildly between speed limits, and the lights always feel longer than they really are. As a result, lots of terrible driving can be viewed on this street at any given time.

It was the first hot day of spring, but not quite summer, and all the college students were out running or playing soccer in the park. I'm headed east to go home. I'm sweaty, cranky, and not paying very much attention to the other drivers around me. I go to merge quickly around a delivery truck and come a little too close to another car. I hear the driver laying on the horn. I wince because I know it's my fault. I hold myself up as a good driver so naturally I'm embarrassed.

I look in the rear view and I see a long dark haired Italianesque man with wrap around black sports sunglasses behind the wheel screaming and cussing. I consider for a moment that maybe he's singing a metal or hip-hop song but he's clearly directing his verbal assault at me. His companion is a bald black man with a crooked smile. He seems to enjoy the tirade his friend is producing. I try to wave apologetically but I realize that there is no real way to convey apology this way without it looking smug. Suddenly he speeds up and pulls around next to me, window down, yelling and pointing. I don't have my window's down so I can't hear him but he's saying *fuck* a lot. I mouth out 'Sorry, my mistake' and somehow, he yells more aggressively. *Never apologize to crazy people*, I remember, immediately curious about the sagacity of this advice.

He begins swerving over towards me quickly as if he's going to hit me and then swerves back at the last second. His friend is laughing and staring me right in the face. I don't react but maintain my speed and position. I'm afraid, and angry that I'm afraid.

This goes on only a short minute before he turns off West End into a car wash with great speed. I'm now angrier and holding it back so I pull over into a gas station to cool down. I begin feeling like a coward for not following or shouting back at him. I keep switching back and forth between rage and reason, wanting to go back and look for him, and reminding myself that there were two of them, and a man like that likely carries a weapon. I carry a pistol myself, but I'm not stupid. I would likely be walking into a severe beating or worse.

I calm down but also decide that I need to gain some power back to alleviate my humiliation. People in this city get worse and worse every day and I'm getting tired of acting so passively. Someone needs to take action.

I drive back down West End, slowly scanning the car wash lot, when I spot the car. It's an older model 2 door Honda that has been put into the beginning stages of conversion into a street racer, and it's not being washed. He must work here. I drive into the lot next door and snap a picture of the car and the license plate, wondering what kind of man this is that is still into street racing aesthetics.

As I'm doing this, I catch a glimpse of him hard at work, and I zoom in to get a poor, but solid photo of him. I feel a little better that I have this information, and that he doesn't know that I have it, so I drive home, knowing that I know where to find him if I ever needed to for some reason.

I could wait a few weeks and deface his car when he gets it painted. He would never know it was me. How could he? This jerk off has no idea that I turned around and took photos. What an absolute moron. I could easily serve up some justice. Just the knowledge that I *could* do something is enough to pacify me. I move on. I have absolutely no intention of really doing anything, but I begin to fantasize.

    A few weeks later, it's Friday afternoon and I'm over on the west side of town, slowly moving through traffic. I'm listening to the news but it's about things I've already heard, so I flip through the stations, unsatisfied with all the music. Eventually I turn it off and take a deep breath. I'm restless and I hate this heat and this traffic. I notice a familiar car a few car lengths up ahead. It;s an older model 2 door Honda with a huge muffler and it's painted a fiery red.

    I wonder if that could be my guy. I had actually forgotten about him until now. I can't tell if it's him, but since I'm free for the day and feeling a bit bored, I decide to follow this car a little while. He stays well ahead of me, and I remember the best way to follow is not too closely. We take some twists and turns through a neighborhood and I see him pull into a condominium complex. As it turns out, I know someone else that lives here too. I consider for a moment that he could be here to see the guy I know, a drug dealer, and I hope so and hope not at the same time.

    I don't pull into the complex. Instead, I drive by it and turn around in a parking lot where I can see down the street to the entrance of the condominiums. I get out and stretch for a moment. After 10 minutes, he doesn't reemerge. I drive in and creep through slowly looking for his car, and I spot it. He's not at the dealers' place. I take a photo of the plate and the door and then I drive away. Later on, I compare my photos and sure enough, it's him. Now I know where he works and where he lives. He has no idea what he's done.

    I sit for a time looking at my photos, wondering why I'm still so compelled to punish this guy. Maybe it's a deep seeded desire for violence or just a sense of control; I reason that it's about justice. Regardless of the motivation, I had a plan in mind. No effort was put into it. It was as if it came from an outside signal broadcast straight into my mind fully formed. As far as I'm concerned, it was divine intervention, telling me to dispense with cosmic will. Who knows how many people this guy has terrorized on the streets. If he acts that way in public, how must he act in private? Punishing him is a favor to society.

------ ,

I spend a couple of weeks periodically driving through the condo complex to get an idea of his schedule. I notice that he's always home consistently on Wednesday nights. I contact a girl I used to date, the one who introduced me to the dealer, and she gives up his contact info way to easily. His name is Antonio. I contact him via text and give him a reminder of when we met. He remembers, and asks what's up. I tell him I'm looking for some weed, that my usual guy was picked up recently, and need a new contact; he says he has some coming in later this weekend. I lie and tell him I'll be out of town and ask if he can hold it until the next Wednesday. He agrees. This'll give me some time to check the patterns one more time.

We confirm plans to meet at his place the next week, smoke, and chill. Perfect, I'll get a little high afterwards; I'll need to. My heart is racing and I start to cough and clear my throat out of the need to do something physical and release the tension. I stand up and pace around my living room, trying to reconcile the actions I'm setting up with my moral compass.

I ask myself if I'm really going to go through with my plan, and as if unconsciously answering my own question I begin to nod yes with my whole body. I've never done anything close to this kind of thing before and I'm scared. But fuck that. It has to be done.

I drive over to the complex around 1am Sunday Morning. Most people are out drinking or already in bed so the lot is sparse. I park next to my guys door and stash an aluminum t-ball bat in the bushes. My roommate had our garage full of boxes from his childhood that his parents had recently dropped off; he would never miss an old t-ball bat. I had also taken a large rock of limestone from the drainage ditch near our house. I stashed this on the side of his building in the bushes as well.

I take some time to walk around to Antonio's lot, making note of the terrain. The time it takes to get from one to the other is about 2 minutes in well-groomed, flat, dry grass. I notice that since I'm not walking on the sidewalk but instead on the edge of the complex there are no street lamps. Perfect. I'm anxious and shaking, but I'm ready.

Wednesday arrives. I drive over to Antonio's a little early and pull in front of his door. I park and wait a bit to make sure no one is around outside. I also want to make sure that Antonio doesn't peer out the window at the sound of my car. I sit still, taking deep breath after deep breath. I ask myself aloud again if I want to do this. It's not too late to turn back. I could just get high with Antonio and call it a night; there's still time.

I decide, and I'm shaking with excitement. I thought I would be more afraid than I really am, but my conviction is firm. As I take one last look around to make sure I'm alone, I put on my leather gloves, and walk through the darkness around to my guy's building. I hesitate. I'm growing more nervous with each step. On last deep breath and a clearing of my throat and I go.

I move quickly and pull out the rock first and I drop it in the grass next to his car. Then I retrieve the bat, propping it up on his driver's side tire. *Moment of Truth*, I thought. I pull down my comically villainous ski mask, pick up the rock, step up on the hood of the car, and with all the power I can manage, I lift the rock behind my head, and pull it forward, slamming it down onto the windshield. It shatters and the car rocks a bit from the impact. The alarm goes off and it's piercing. I didn't expect it to be so loud. *I'm in it now.*

The porch light turns on as I hop down and grab the bat, my knuckles white inside the glove. My heart is going to explode and I swallow hard. I think for a brief moment that I'm not sure how big he is compared to me. I take a few steps away and stand in the dark to wait. The moment he opens the door he runs out to look at the damage, a look of confusion and disbelief mixed with rage. He has a pistol in his hand. *Strike!*

I emerge into the light as fast as I can and bring the bat down hard on his wrist holding the gun and it drops in the grass. He lunges backwards and screams in what must be a mix of pain and surprise. He never saw me coming.

I can feel myself smiling under the mask, adrenaline pumping full force at having disarmed him so easily. I was lucky, no doubt. I quickly kick the gun away under his car and stand tall, arms open, inviting him to come at me. I can see in his face that he's as blood drunk as I am and I lick my lips with anticipation of the coming collision.

He goes. I side step and as he loses balance. I shoulder check him onto the hood of his car. While he is off kilter, I take another deep breath and swing the bat right into the back of one of his knees. He screams, rolls over on his back, and slides to the ground. *He had one chance to get at me and he blew it. Pity.*

I switch positions and I swing and hit the other knee as hard as I can. I hear how clean it breaks. He screams again, this time louder. I can see other lights coming on around the complex. My whole body is in flex and I'm breathing short but remain fully alert. I toss the bat far into the bushes. My heart is going to beat out of my chest and I burp loudly releasing the tension.

He's now crying uncontrollably, and I realize the damage to his car is minimal to the damage of his knees. He looks up at me, terrified, and I kick him once in the mouth with my heel. He spits blood. I tell him that he knows what he did and briskly walk away into the darkness.

Later on, he'll see that I had scrawled a message into the rock, *"you cheating bastard"*. I think he has a regular girlfriend but I'm not certain. I also don't know that he's the cheating type, but I assume so based on his driving behavior.

If I'm wrong and he's a good and faithful lover, then my hope is that between my parting words and this message, he'll assume the attack was meant for someone else. No matter what, any girlfriend he has will be suspicious enough to make things bad for him emotionally as time goes on. I just hope he's smart enough to take the necessary lessons from this encounter.

I bolt through the edge of the complex, and stop at the corner of Antonio's to catch my bearings and burp again. I feel nauseous and my mind flashes back to my guy on the ground screaming, the sound of his knee breaking, and the blood being spit out. I pull off the mask and throw up into it a little, just enough to spit and leave a bad taste. I have to laugh as I start to feel sweat between my legs and my pants. For a moment, I thought I was getting a bit of an erection. I didn't realize it would affect me in such physical ways. The whole act took maybe 3 minutes but I can feel that I'll remember it for the rest of my life. Sirens ring in the distance. I toss the mask and gloves in my trunk, change my shoes, and compose myself the best I can, forcing more burps in an effort to amp myself down.

I knock at Antonio's door and I'm invited in with warm greetings. I use the toilet, gargle some water, splash some on my face, and head back to the living room to get high and watch Game of Thrones. The place is filthy and after only a couple of minutes, it's clear to me that Antonio is likely into some harder shit than I was expecting. Maybe that was why I got his info so easily; he's not afraid of who knows his business. He is scary and very confident. He's also reckless and not as smart as he thinks. He should probably be off the streets. I have absolutely no intention of doing anything, but I begin to fantasize.

NOTES

NOTES

Acknowledgements:

Alexander Schmid, Bennett Tansey, Matthew Cook, David Oldham, Ty Kun, Emiko Saito, Laurel Lieb, Janet Lim, X.A. Alexander, Adam Lane Smith, Damon Heard, and Stu Mentha.

Thank you all or your feedback, suggestions, edits, criticisms, and support.

J. Friedrich Allyn is a native of the American South.

He enjoys: motion, order, aphorisms, history, language, myth, legend, symbolism, maps, planning, spreadsheets, sunlight, wind, fire, thunder, lightning, ice, landscapes, cliffs, waves, hollows, foxes, flamboyant birds, castles, alleyways, courtyards, highways, jeeps, trains, tall wooden ships, axes, archery, field watches, dark chocolate, bold cigars, instrumental surf music, bass guitars, floor toms, weightlifting, boots, winter scarfs, felt tip pens, stainless steel, the color orange, obedient dogs, and kind women with expressive faces.

If you enjoyed this work, J. Friedrich Allyn Recommends:

Yukio Mishima:
Acts of Worship
Death in Midsummer & Other Stories

Flannery O'Conner:
A Good Man is Hard to Find and Other Stories
Everything That Rises Must Converge

James Joyce:
Dubliners

Fyodor Dostoevsky:
A Weak Heart
An Honest Thief
A Christmas Tree and a Wedding
White Nights
A Little Hero
A Nasty Story
The Crocodile
The Heavenly Christmas Tree
A Gentle Creature
The Peasant Marey
The Dream of a Ridiculous Man